Merry Sam

Love you always,
Grandpa &
Grandma

Through her passion and simplicity, Cathy has given every person a way to explain a complicated theological truth (the Trinity) in a way both kids *and* adults can understand. But it is more than just a book about a snowman or the Trinity–it is an invitation to every reader to know Jesus as the forgiver of their souls and leader of their lives! Thank you for this book. I will never look at a snowman the same way!

—Darrell White,
Senior Pastor,
Sheridan Wesleyan Church

A Snowman's Gift

Cathy Slikker-Vlahos

TATE PUBLISHING & Enterprises

Published by Tate Publishing & Enterprises, LLC
127 E. Trade Center Terrace | Mustang, Oklahoma 73064 USA
1.888.361.9473 | www.tatepublishing.com

Tate Publishing is committed to excellence in the publishing industry. The company reflects the philosophy established by the founders, based on Psalm 68:11,
"The Lord gave the word and great was the company of those who published it."

Book design copyright © 2010 by Tate Publishing, LLC. All rights reserved.
Cover and Interior design by Michael Lee
Illustration by Kathy Hoyt

Published in the United States of America

ISBN: 978-1-61663-142-0
Religion: Christian Education: Children & Youth
10.04.20

Dedication

I thank God for allowing me to pen this story. I enjoy explaining how wonderful God is to my children every day of our lives. Thanks to my loving, supportive husband, Ted P. Vlahos. He gave you to me! To my children: my true blessings from God, you bring to mind wonderful God-teaching moments. Drew and Jenna, I love you so much! My prayer for you has always been that you become spiritually mature adults. Colton, Lexie, and Walker: you are truly wonderful children to have in my life. I pray God blesses our lives together as we grow in love. Thank you for allowing me to share our stories.

Illustrations inspired by Walker James Vlahos

Acknowledgements

Thank you to the numerous family and friends who took the time to read and encourage me to try to have this story published. Thanks for the gentle push of my dear friend, Vicki Jost, who said "God's will is 100% - submit it! It will be published if he wills." A number of God's agents (pastors and friends) took time from their busy schedules to help me edit this story. These include Jordan Patterson, my first outside editor. In addition, Sam Lewis, Darrell White, Laura Welty and Dan Ziebarth, thanks for your time. A special thanks to Michele Halseide, a newfound friend who graciously assisted in refining this book. Thank you to Tate Publishing for believing in this message and giving it life!

Introduction

The concept of the Trinity can be complicated to explain to adults, not to mention children. Therefore, the story of the snowman is designed to simply explain the Trinity as we incorporate a fun story of how we build a snowman. God's word tells us to teach our children as we walk along in every day life.

Teach them [God's words and principles] to your children, talking about them [God's words and principles] when you sit at home and when you walk along the road, when you lie down and when you get up.
Deuteronomy 11:19 (NIV)

Please join me as we build our snowman and explain how wonderful our God truly is!

It was a snowy, Sunday winter afternoon and the snowflakes were huge! It was hard to see between them. The snowflakes were gently falling to the ground like feathers from a torn pillow. "Look, Daddy," Jenna exclaimed, "every snowflake is so beautiful."

"And good to eat," her father added, "like miniature snow cones. Why don't you go outside and catch some snowflakes on your tongue. I'll give you a penny for every one you catch!"

Jenna's eyes widened and danced with anticipation. "Please, Mommy, please will you come with me?" Jenna's mom couldn't resist. So they bundled up nice and warm thanks to their furry hats, thick gloves, and of course, fleece-lined boots. Off they went, Jenna and mom, into the wet, white, cold outdoors, catching snowflakes on their tongues.

Before long Jenna bent down to scoop up some snow. In a flash she'd formed a snowball and was hurling it at her mom, who quickly returned fire. "Snowball fight!" Jenna declared. Snowballs flew back and forth like missiles. It was great! Playing in the snow was so much fun!

"Truce, truce!" her mother finally called out. "You win! Let's use our snowball-making skills to build a snowman instead. Come on; let's make a huge snowball for the snowman's bottom." Jenna watched as her mother showed her how to roll and pack the snow.

Jenna said, "It's my turn." She carefully rolled and packed and tumbled and smacked the snow after each roll.

Very quickly the snowball became too big for Jenna to roll. Jenna's face got increasingly red as she tried and tried to roll the giant white ball over. Jenna would *not* allow her mother to help. She finally pushed it over on her fourth try. Yes, the fourth try; but she did it herself! "Keep packing the snow," her mother said. "If we don't pack the snow hard enough, the snowman will crumble." So Jenna worked even harder to smooth and pack the snowball. It was a perfect bottom! "You know," her mom added, "the snowman is much like us. If we don't have a strong foundation, we, too, will crumble and fall." Jenna began to laugh, "So how do we pack our bottoms?"

"Well, think about how a house is built. Before any walls go up, the builders pour a foundation of cement that dries and becomes solid, like rock." Her mother said. "So how do I build my life upon rock?" Jenna asked. "That's easy," mom responded. "You build it on God and his guiding principles. He is the foundation of our life and the rock we can stand firm on. So you see, without God our life will crumble."

"I don't get it, Mom. How do I do that? I can pack a snowball, but I really don't know how to build my life on God," Jenna admitted. Her mother explained, "Jesus once said: *Therefore everyone who hears these words of mine [Jesus] and puts them into practice is like a wise man who built his house on the rock [a solid foundation]* (Matthew 7:24, NIV).

"Putting God's words and guiding principles into practice is kind of like building the base of our snowman. To build our big snowball, we roll it over and over in the snow. It's the same with our lives; we keep rolling our lives over and over in God's words. You pack down the truth until you become firm and solid in your beliefs and faith. Then we will have a solid foundation that we can stand on. Jenna blurted, "I still don't get it, Mom. How do I roll in God's words?"

"You read the Bible, silly," Mom responded. "And you go to church where people help you understand what you're reading. Did you know that God actually promises in Ecclesiastes 2:26 that, 'God gives wisdom, knowledge and happiness?' So, sweetheart, do you understand God is our foundation? His words of truth tell us how to live our lives in the very best way!"

Her mother explained that God is not only our foundation, but the Bible tells us that God created the world, the foundation we all live on, and he created you!

In the beginning God created the heavens and the earth.
Genesis 1:1 (NIV)

Then God said, "Let us make man [you!] in our image in our likeness [God's image; so we are like him!]..."
Genesis 1:26 (NIV)

"Mom, I know we go to church, and I learn a little about God each week. But help me understand him." Jenna urged.

"The Bible says that God is not a man, he has a forever love for us, he always tells the truth, never changes his mind, and is slow to get angry with us," explained her mother.

The Lord [God] is slow to anger, abounding in love [a never ending love] and forgiving sin and rebellion [forgiving our bad choices].
                                        Numbers 14:18 (NIV)

God is not a man, that he should lie, [he cannot and will never lie] nor a son of man, that he should change his mind [His word, the Bible, is true and will not change].
                                        Numbers 23:19 (NIV)

Now it was time to roll the middle snowball for her snowman. Once again, Jenna rolled and packed and tumbled and smacked the snow. Her hands became cold and red so she went inside to change gloves. When she stepped back out into the white powdery fluff, she helped her mother lift the middle of her snowman. It was heavy! Jenna said she was glad she did not have to lift the big bottom snowball. Her mother laughed in agreement. Jenna's mother told her that if the snowman were real, that the middle would hold his heart. She said that the Son of God, Jesus, was given to us to offer us forgiveness and to change our hearts. "That's another thing I don't get," Jenna told her mom. "Why and how does he change our hearts?"

"God wants us to have a pure and clean heart like his. So God sent His Son, Jesus, who lived on earth to show us what God's heart is like. You see, when we ask Jesus to change us, he does it from the inside out. So when we make bad choices and disobey his principles, it saddens him and keeps our hearts from being like his. But when we tell Jesus we are sorry for what we've done wrong, Jesus forgives us–always–every time! This is how he cleans and changes our hearts with the power of his Spirit. God and Jesus have forgiving hearts full of love and service. Wouldn't you like to have a heart like that?" asked her mother.

> For God, who said, "Let light shine out of darkness," made his light shine in our hearts to give us the light of knowledge of the glory of God [God's heart] in the face of Christ [Jesus].
> 2 Corinthians 4:6 (NIV)

> Every good and perfect gift is from above, coming down from the Father of the heavenly lights, who does not change like shifting shadows.
> James 1:17 (NIV)

"What a great gift! You see Jenna; the gift is Jesus! So when we ask him to come into our lives, forgive us, and change our hearts, he gives us the power to make better choices. He removes the bad feelings from our hearts for our wrong choices. Then we will feel new and white as snow," her mother said.

> Wash me and I will be whiter than snow.
> Psalm 51: 7 (NIV)

> Though your sins are like scarlet, they shall be as white as snow.
> Isaiah 1:18 (NIV)

Her mother explained that when Jesus left heaven to come to earth as a man, he lived a perfect life to teach us how to live. Jenna asked, "Why would he want to leave heaven?"

"Because God asked him to do that job so we could go to heaven one day," her mom replied.

"What job?" Jenna said.

"Jesus showed us how to live and then he had to die for our sins (our bad choices and attitudes) on the cross, but he rose from the dead three days later and conquered death."

> Christ Jesus, who had destroyed death and has brought life...
> 2 Timothy 1:10 (NIV)

"Jesus now sits at the right hand of God."

> It saves you by the resurrection of Jesus Christ, who has gone into heaven and is at God's right hand—with angels, authorities, and powers in submission to him.
> 1 Peter 3:21–22 (NIV)

Jenna asked, "Why did Jesus die on the cross?"

Her mother said, "In Romans 4:25, the Bible says, 'He was delivered over to death for our sins and was raised to life for our justification [to make us look perfect to God].' He died to pay for our sins (bad choices) so that we could go to heaven to be with him forever. God wants *all* of us to live with him in heaven after we die. All we need to do to get into heaven is to love Jesus just like he loves us."

> Jesus answered, 'I am the way and the truth and the life. No one comes to the Father (God) except through me.'
> John 14:6 (NIV)

Jenna was trying to put together all the new thoughts her mother had given her. She continued working hard to build her snowman. Her face was red, the hair coming out from under her hat was wet, but her boots, covered with snow, kept her toes nice and warm. She rolled and packed and tumbled and smacked the snow again to make the head of her snowman. She gathered rocks for his eyes, a carrot for his nose, and asparagus for his smile. "Now the snowman seems to have come alive!" Jenna bragged. "Do you think he would be smart and wise?" Mom said with a smile. "Well now we have the head that represents the Holy Spirit of God, who guides our thoughts and helps us make good decisions. He gives us direction, but he can not do his job of guiding unless we have invited Jesus into our lives."

Jenna asked, "Where does the Holy Spirit come from?" Her mother said that God gives him to us.

> God has poured out his love into our hearts by the Holy Spirit, whom he has given us.
>
> Romans 5:5 (NIV)

Jenna again asked, "Who gets the Holy Spirit?" Her mother told her that all you have to do is just ask God! In Luke 11:13 it says, "Your Father in heaven gives the Holy Spirit to those who ask him!"

Jenna said with a puzzled look on her face, "What does he do?"

"Well the Bible tells us that he guides and teaches us," said her mother.

> But the counselor, the Holy Spirit, whom the Father [God] will send in my name [Jesus] will teach you all things and will remind you of everything I [Jesus] have said to you [God's Word: The Bible].
>
> John 14: 26 (NIV)

> But when he, the Spirit of truth comes, he will guide you into all truth…
>
> John 16:13 (NIV)

Jenna again asked with her eyes wide open, "What will he give us?"

Her mother said, "He gives us great things that are sometimes hard to appreciate and keep in our lives. The Bible says, in Galatians 5:22–23, 'But the fruit of the Spirit is love, joy, peace, patience, kindness, goodness, faithfulness, gentleness and self control.'"

Then Jenna's eyes grew wide with excitement. "Now I get it, Mom! You mean that, like the snowman that has three parts—a bottom, middle, and head,—God is made of three parts: God, Jesus, and the Holy Spirit."

"That's right!" Jenna's mother replied. "A snowman cannot be a snowman without his head or his middle. God would not be complete if we did not have God the Father who created and loves us, Jesus, God the Son who saves us from our sin, and God the Holy Spirit who guides us into living out the principles God wants us to live. Jenna stared into the snowman's eyes for a long time and finally remarked, "Snowman, you have really helped me understand God."

May the grace of the Lord Jesus Christ, and the love of God, and the fellowship of the Holy Spirit be with you all.
2 Corinthians 13:14 (NIV)

Jenna's mother overheard her remark and said smiling, "Understanding God is the Snowman's gift to you. Just remember that the big difference between God and a snowman is that God is alive and his love never melts or goes away. God promises us in Joshua 1:5: 'I will never leave you nor forsake you.'"

The sun grew warmer and warmer with each passing day. Jenna went out to her snowman every day. By the third day, he had melted. Jenna's heart was sad for she had worked so hard to put him together. As she turned to walk back to her mother, she noticed a beautiful purple crocus flower coming up between patches of snow—the first flower of spring. The flower made her smile, but she ran to her mother looking for reassurance and said, "Why will God never leave us?" Her mother said, "Because he made us and loves us so much that he wants us with him forever!"

For God so loved the world that he gave his one and only son [Jesus], that whoever believe in him shall not perish but have eternal life [in heaven with God].

John 3:16 (NIV)

She said that God's word says that nothing can keep us from the love of God.

For I am convinced that neither death nor life, neither angel nor demons, neither the present nor the future, nor any powers, neither height nor depth, nor anything else in all creation, will be able to separate us from the love of God that is in Christ Jesus our Lord.

Romans 8:38–39 (NIV)

"So if we are going to be with God forever, where will we be?" Jenna asked.

Her mother said, "God has prepared a forever home for us called heaven. In heaven we will walk on streets of gold. What do you think that will be like?"

Jenna said, "I'm not sure. I wonder how shiny and bright they will be."

> In my Father's house [God's house] are many rooms; if it were not so, I [Jesus] would have told you. I [Jesus] am going there to prepare a place for you.
>
> John 14:2 (NIV)

> The great street of the city was of pure gold, like transparent glass.
>
> Revelation 21:21 (NIV)

"I'm not sure either, sweetheart, so we will have to wait until Jesus comes and gets us. While we wait, we need to love Jesus just like he loves us." Jenna's mother added, "Until then, Jesus is sitting at the right hand of God, but the Holy Spirit is with us, helping us make good decisions every day as we pray to God for directions for our life."

That evening, as Jenna's mother tucked her into bed, Jenna said her prayers. She thanked God for loving her. She prayed that the Holy Spirit would help her to make good decisions every day. She asked the Holy Spirit to teach her God's guidelines for life, to help her follow them, and to show her what to do in her life. She thanked God for Jesus dying on the cross. She asked to be forgiven for her wrong decisions so she could one day go to heaven to be with him forever.

As her mother left her room, Jenna said, "I love you mom. Thanks for the snowman!"

Additional Supporting Scripture
for Parents to Share with their Children
as they Deem Appropriate

God/Our Foundation:

He [God] who is the Glory of Israel does not lie or change his mind; for he is not a man, that he should change his mind.
1 Samuel 15:29 (NIV)

You [God] are gracious and compassionate God, slow to anger and abounding in love, a God who relents from sending calamity.
Jonah 4:2 (NIV)

God has said, "Never will I leave you, never will I forsake you."
Hebrews 13:5 (NIV)

For no one can lay any foundation other than the one already laid, which is Jesus Christ [God's son Jesus became a man and walked on earth to teach us how to live and paid the price for our sins].
1 Corinthians 3:11 (NIV)

The church of the living God, the pillar and foundation of the truth.
1 Timothy 3:15 (NIV)

Repent [turn away from our bad decisions], then, and turn to God, so that your sins may be wiped out.
Acts 3:19 (NIV)

But God demonstrates his own love for us in this: While we were still sinners, Christ [Jesus Christ] died for us.
Romans 5:8 (NIV)

Don't you know that you yourselves are God's temple and that God's Spirit lives in you?
1 Corinthians 3:16 (NIV)

Our Hearts:

God sent the Spirit of his Son [Jesus] into our hearts.

Galatians 4:6 (NIV)

But your hearts must be fully committed to the Lord our God, to live by his decrees and obey his commands, as at this time.

1 Kings 8:61 (NIV)

Trust in the Lord with all your heart and lean not on your own understanding; in all your ways acknowledge him, and he will make your paths straight.

Proverbs 3:5–6 (NIV)

That if you confess with your mouth, "Jesus is Lord," and believe in your heart that God raised him from the dead, you will be saved. For it is with your heart that you believe and are justified, and it is with your mouth that you confess and are saved.

Romans 10:9–10 (NIV)

All the prophets testify about him [Jesus] that everyone who believes in him receives forgiveness of sins through his [Jesus's] name.

Acts 10:43 (NIV)

Your kingdom [heaven] is an everlasting kingdom…The Lord [God] is faithful to all his promises and loving toward all he has made [you!].

Psalm 145:13 (NIV)

My purpose is that they may be encouraged in heart and united in love, so that they may have the full riches of complete understanding, in order they may know the mystery of God, namely, Christ, in whom are hidden all the treasures of wisdom and knowledge.

Colossians 2:2–3 (NIV)

May the Lord direct your hearts into God's love and Christ's perseverance [His life].

2 Thessalonians 3:5 (NIV)

Jesus lives and paid the price for our sin:

That Christ died for our sins according to the scriptures, that he was buried, that he was raised on the third day according to the scriptures, and that he appeared to Peter, and then to the twelve. After that he appeared to more than five hundred of the brothers at the same time.

1 Corinthians 15:3–6 (NIV)

After his [Jesus's] suffering, he showed himself to these men and gave many convincing proofs that he was alive. He appeared to them over a period of forty days and spoke about the kingdom of God [Heaven].

Acts 1:3 (NIV)

He [Jesus] told them, "This is what is written: The Christ will suffer and rise from the dead on the third day…"

Luke 24:46 (NIV)

He himself [Jesus] bore our sins in his body on the tree, [the cross] so that we might die to sins and live for righteousness; by his wounds you have been healed [He was beaten for our sake].

1 Peter 2:24 (NIV)

For Christ died for sins once for all, the righteous for the unrighteous, to bring you to God. He was put to death in the body but made alive by the Spirit.

1 Peter 3:18 (NIV)

When you were dead in your sins and in the uncircumcision of your sinful nature, God made you alive with Christ. He forgave us all our sins, having canceled the written code, with its regulations, that was against us and that stood opposed to us; he took it away, nailing it to the cross.

Colossians 2:13–14 (NIV)

God made him [Jesus] who had no sin to be sin for us, so that in him we might become the righteousness of God.

2 Corinthians 5:21 (NIV)

He [Jesus] appeared so that he might take away our sins. And in him is no sin.

1 John 3:5 (NIV)

We know also that the Son of God [Jesus] has come and has given us understanding, so that we may know him who is true. And we are in him who is true–even in his Son Jesus Christ. He is the true God and eternal life.

1 John 5:20 (NIV)

The Son is the radiance of God's glory and the exact representation of his being, sustaining all things by his powerful word. After he had provided purification for sins, he sat down at the right hand of the Majesty in heaven.

Hebrews 1:3 (NIV)

Holy Spirit:

God is spirit, and his worshipers [us] must worship in spirit and in truth.

John 4:24 (NIV)

Peter replied, "Repent [turn from your bad decisions] and be baptized, every one of you, in the name of Jesus Christ for the forgiveness of your sins. And you will receive the gift of the Holy Spirit.

Acts 2:38 (NIV)

In the same way, the Spirit helps us in our weakness. We do not know what we ought to pray for, but the Spirit himself intercedes [talks to God] for us with groans that words cannot express [when we do not know what to say to God].

Romans 8:26 (NIV)

But God has revealed it to us by his Spirit. The Spirit searches all things, even the deep things of God. For who among men knows the thoughts of a man except the man's spirit within him? In the same way no one knows the thoughts of God except the Spirit of God.

1 Corinthians 2:10–11 (NIV)

Dear Reader, *Samson, Emery*

Thank you for taking the time to read this story. My prayer for you is found in Jude 20-21 (NIV):

But you, dear friends, build yourselves up in your most holy faith and pray in the Holy Spirit. Keep yourselves in God's love as you wait for the mercy of our Lord, Jesus Christ, to bring you to eternal life.

Sincerely,
Cathy,
A Sister in Christ

May God abundantly bless your life as you understand Him more!

Cathy

e|LIVE

listen|imagine|view|experience

AUDIO BOOK DOWNLOAD INCLUDED WITH THIS BOOK!

In your hands you hold a complete digital entertainment package. Besides purchasing the paper version of this book, this book includes a free download of the audio version of this book. Simply use the code listed below when visiting our website. Once downloaded to your computer, you can listen to the book through your computer's speakers, burn it to an audio CD or save the file to your portable music device (such as Apple's popular iPod) and listen on the go!

How to get your free audio book digital download:

1. Visit www.tatepublishing.com and click on the e|LIVE logo on the home page.
2. Enter the following coupon code:
   0ca9-b8b2-a5ac-e554-b77d-fc67-2e8f-ddc8
3. Download the audio book from your e|LIVE digital locker and begin enjoying your new digital entertainment package today!